The Perfect Birthday

By Celestine Greene

Illustrations By Clarence G. Moore

Guyton-Moore Strategic Services LLC
Publishing Division

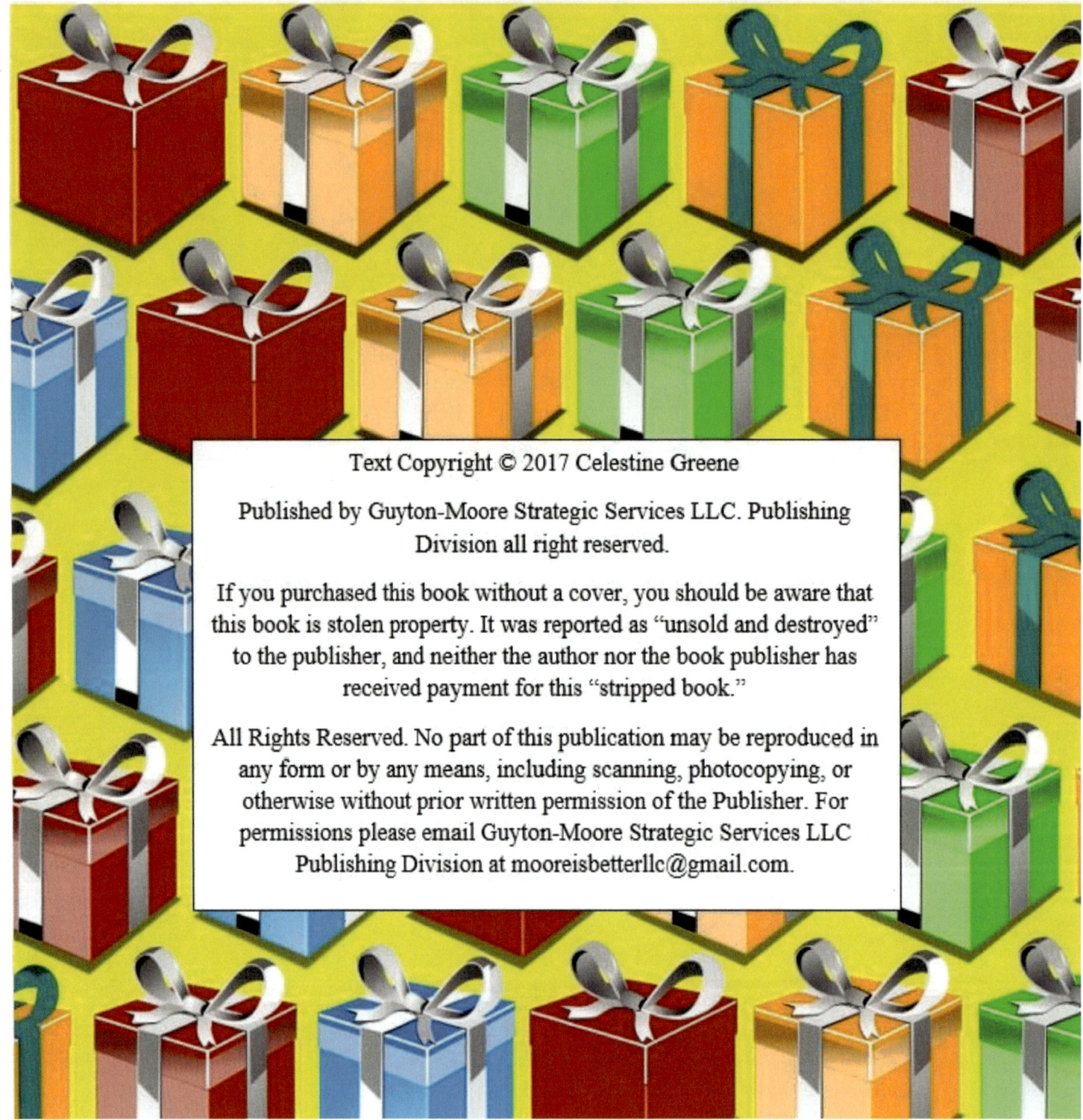

Text Copyright © 2017 Celestine Greene

Published by Guyton-Moore Strategic Services LLC. Publishing Division all right reserved.

If you purchased this book without a cover, you should be aware that this book is stolen property. It was reported as "unsold and destroyed" to the publisher, and neither the author nor the book publisher has received payment for this "stripped book."

All Rights Reserved. No part of this publication may be reproduced in any form or by any means, including scanning, photocopying, or otherwise without prior written permission of the Publisher. For permissions please email Guyton-Moore Strategic Services LLC Publishing Division at mooreisbetterllc@gmail.com.

One rainy day Annie was sitting in her room wondering what she wanted for her birthday.

"What would you like for your birthday Annie?" Her mother said as she entered Annie's bedroom.

"I do not know mom," Annie replied.

"I have an idea," said her mom. "Let's go to the mall and maybe you will see something special for your birthday."

"Okay, can we pick up cousin Eva?" Annie replied with a smile and a twinkle in her eye.

"Yes we can," Mom replied.

After Mom made breakfast, Annie ate her food quickly. Then they picked up cousin Eva and drove to the mall.

When they got to the mall they saw all kinds of stores. They saw shoe stores.

As they were leaving the mall they passed a pet store.
There were two puppy dogs playing in the window.
"Look at the puppies in the window!" Annie shouted.

Annie asked the pet shop owner to hold the black puppy and Eva wanted to hold the white puppy.

They both fell in love with the puppies.

"I would love to have this puppy for my birthday. He is so cute." Annie said to Eva.

"Would you like to take the puppy home?" The shop owner asked.

"Yes, yes, yes! I will ask my Mom." replied Annie excited as she ran over to her mom. "Mom, can I have this puppy for my birthday?"

"We will see," said her mother.

Annie went to sleep that night and dreamed about the cute puppy she saw in the pet store.

She dreamed of him fetching a ball. She dreamed of walking him in the park.

The next morning Annie woke up early. She was still thinking about the puppy. Suddenly her mother walked in with a big pink box.

"Happy birthday, Annie." Her mother said.

Annie jumped out of bed and started opening the box when all of a sudden, the puppy jumped up and licked her on the cheek.

"Oh mother, what a perfect birthday surprise. Thank you!" Said Annie. "I love you Mom and I love this puppy!" Annie hugged her mother then picked up the puppy.

She was so excited she did not know what to do first, so she just sat in her favorite chair and held the puppy until he jumped out of her arms onto the floor.

"This is the happiest day of my life," said Annie.

"I would like to take my puppy for a walk," said Annie.

"We must go back to the pet shop to buy some supplies for the puppy first," said Annie's mother.

"Mom, where is the puppy?" Annie asked.

Then Annie heard a scratch on the closet door. When Annie opened it, out popped the puppy with her shoe in his mouth. Annie laughed and picked him up. Her Mom laughed also.

"Remember he is very young and you must watch him," Annie's mom said.

Off they went to the pet shop. The pet shop owner greeted Annie and her Mom at the door and handed them a list of supplies to care for the puppy.

Annie's mom put the leash on the new puppy and walked out of the pet shop.

"What will we call the puppy?" Asked Annie's mom.

"I think I will call him Money," answered Annie.

"That is a funny name for a puppy. Why do you want to name him Money?" Annie's mom asks.

"I heard you and the pet shop owner talk about how much money it will cost to care for the puppy and I thought that would be a nice name for him," Annie said.

"That is how Money got his name. Come on Money let's go play fetch," Annie said with excitement.

"The Perfect Birthday" was inspired by a true story about a little girl named Annie who did not know what she wanted for her birthday. Her mother took her to the shopping mall to look at birthday ideas.

Questions

1. What color was the new puppy?

2. What did Annie name the puppy?

3. What did Money take out of the closet?

Made in the USA
Columbia, SC
17 June 2017